Tog the Dog

Colin and Jacqui Hawkins

DORLING KINDERSLEY
London • New York • Stuttgart

Have you heard of Tog the dog?

d

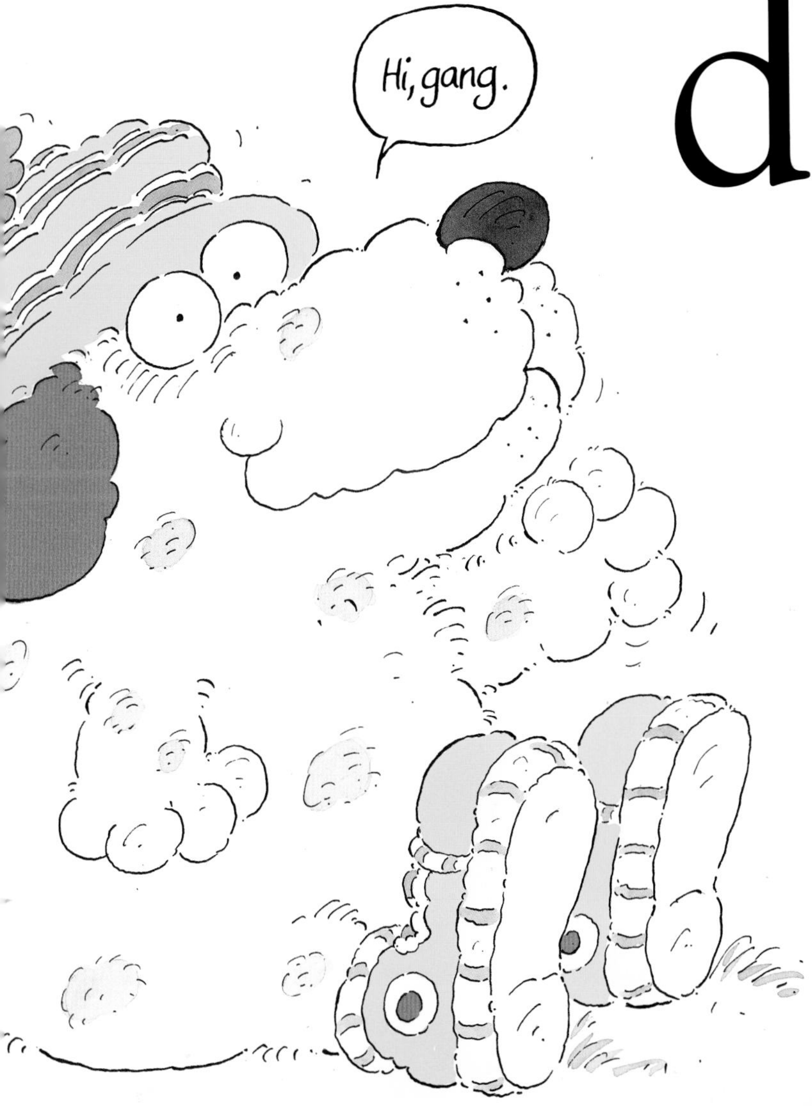

One day Tog went out
for a jog.

He got lost in a fog,

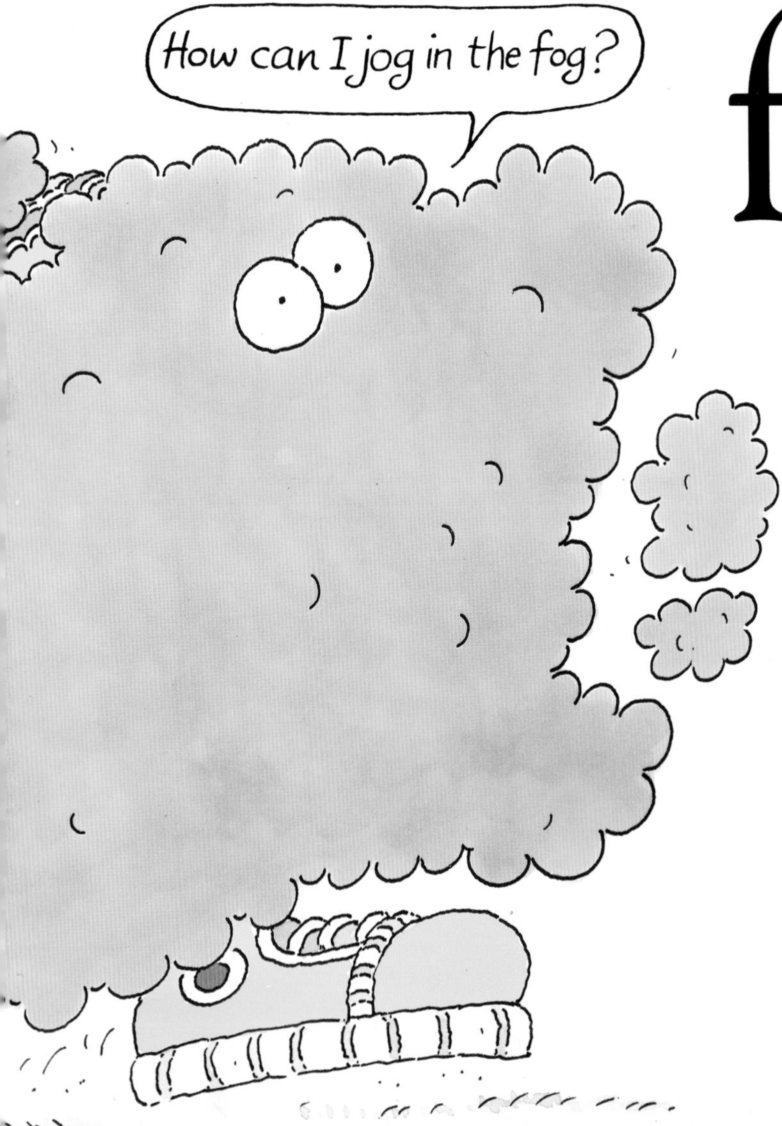

f

tripped over a cog,

fell into a bog,

b

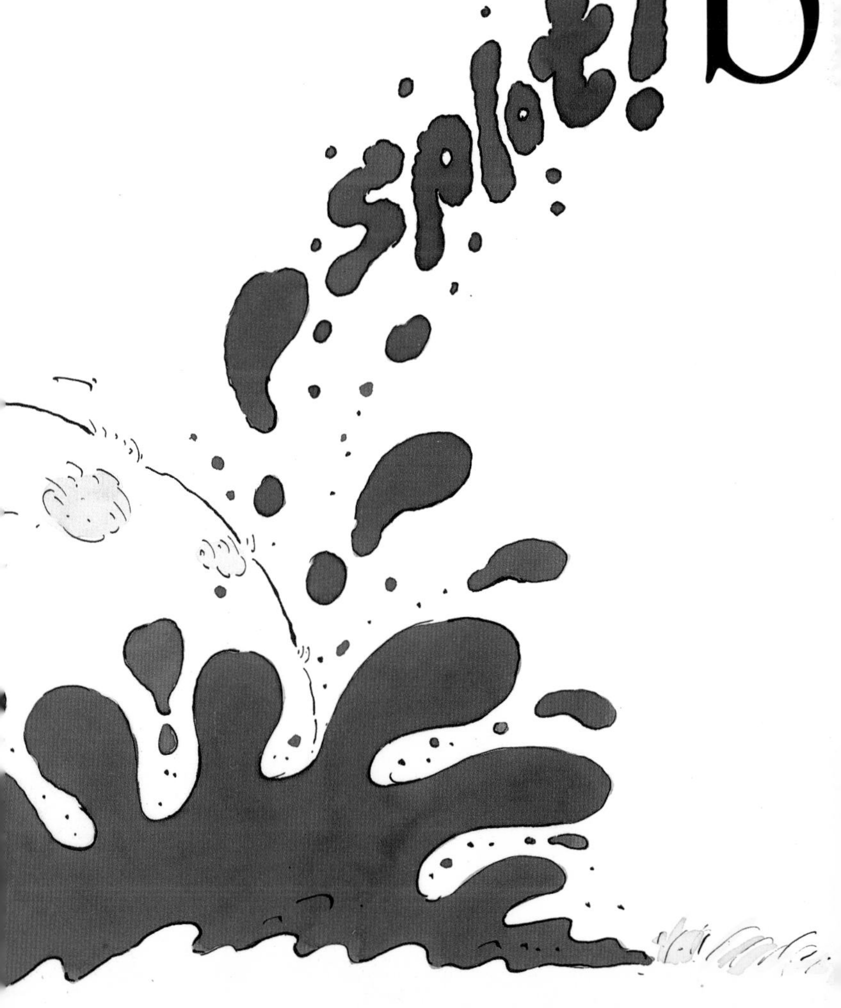

and frightened a frog.

fr

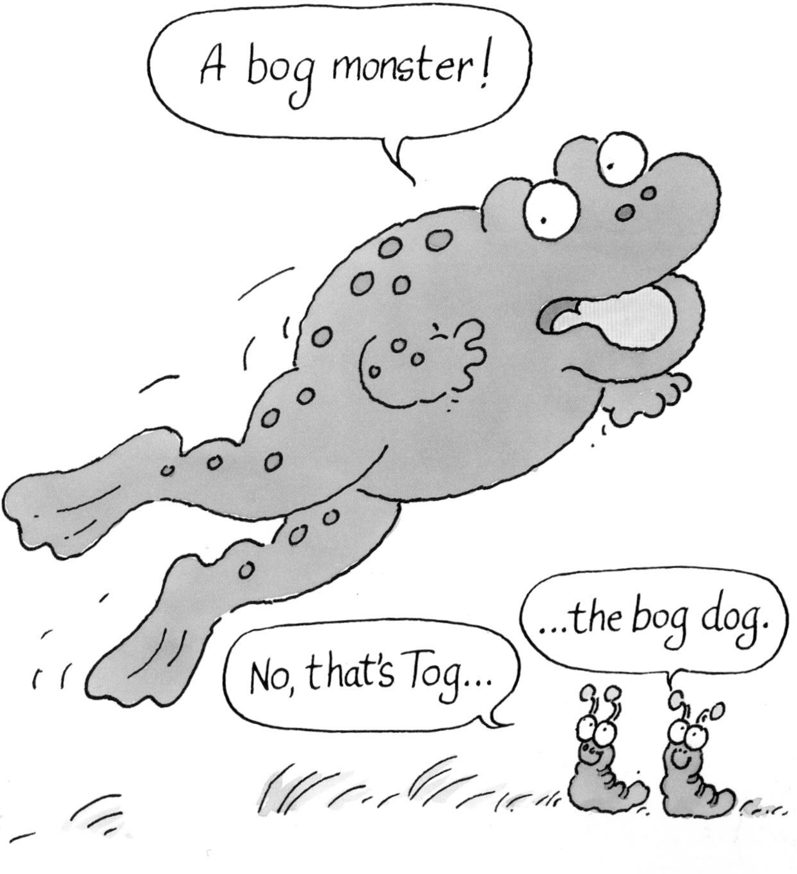

Along came a fat hog,

h

who picked up a log,

1

and pulled out of the bog
the dog called Tog.

Now, Tog, you're out of the bog.

Tog

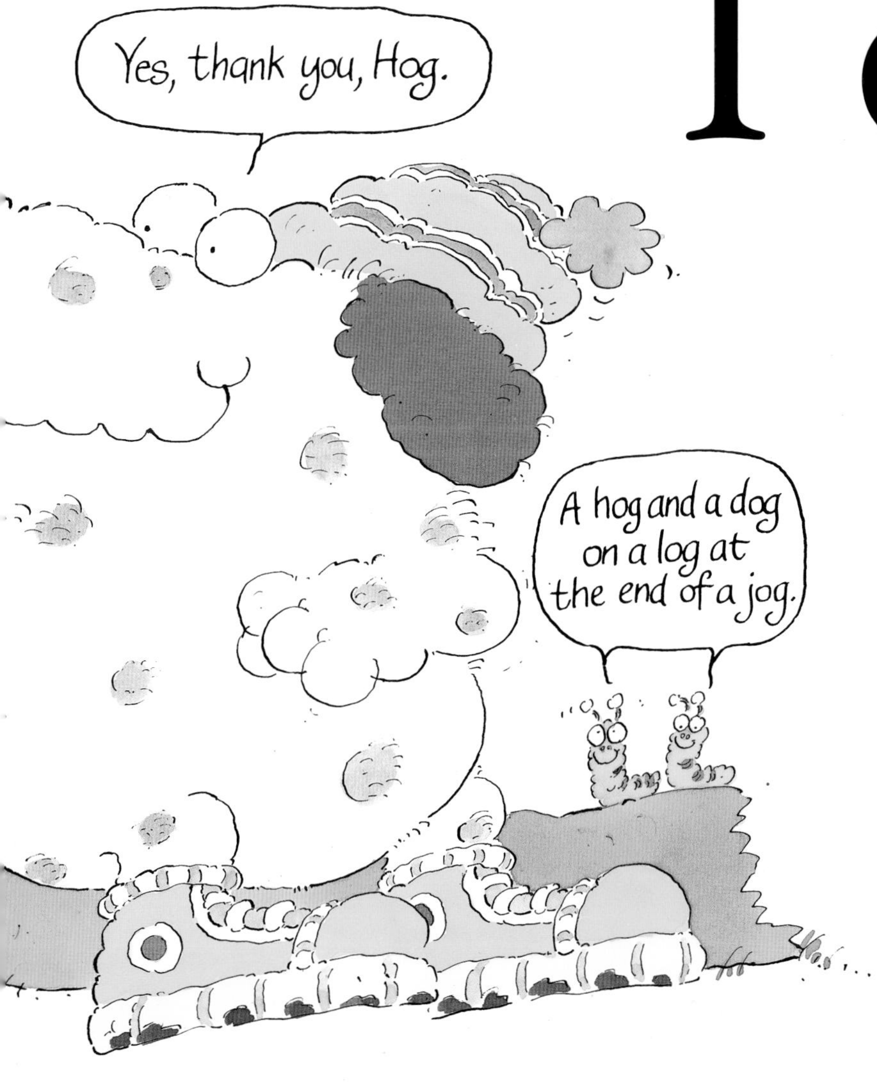

A DORLING KINDERSLEY BOOK

Published in the United Kingdom in 1995
by Dorling Kindersley Limited,
9 Henrietta Street, London WC2E 8PS
Reprinted 1996
Published in the United States in 1995
by Dorling Kindersley Publishing, Inc.,
95 Madison Avenue, New York, New York 10016

4 6 8 10 9 7 5 3

ISBN 0-7513-5353-1 (UK)
ISBN 0-7894-0176-2 (US)

Reproduction by DOT Gradations
Printed in Italy by L.E.G.O.